RED CRANE

David N. Alderman

PROLOGUE

D etective Hale cut through the strips of yellow and black police tape and jimmied the lock on the door to Apartment 111. He pushed the door open a crack as the stench of cigarette smoke and rot blew into his face, making his stomach turn. He stepped into the apartment, exchanging the warmth of the hallway for the cold chill of a crime scene that was only hours old.

He quietly shut the door behind him, hopeful none of the neighbors had seen him enter. The department knew nothing of his presence here. He had been ordered to stay far away from this particular crime scene, but he had no idea why. He wasn't a suspect, and this part of Jameson was under his jurisdiction.

Moonlight pierced the long vertical blinds that hung over the living room window, casting white stripes across the disheveled studio apartment. The only sounds traveling through the small living space were the humming of the heater in the apartment next door and the sound of a raucous party in the apartment below Hale's feet.

He made his way past the small kitchen to his right and entered the living area. The broken lamp on the floor told him he wasn't going to get the light he wanted for his investigation. The toppled sectional couch told him somebody with some

3

degree of strength had been here, probably looking for something. And the smashed wooden computer desk told him there had been an intense struggle, one he knew hadn't ended well.

He stepped over the broken pieces of the desk and approached the window, opening the blinds. The moonlight poured across him, filling the room as he stared out from the twentieth floor on the city of Jameson. The twinkling lights of the city attempted to charm him with their wiles, to convince him it was the summation of something more than filth and degradation and crime. But Detective Hale had been charmed too many times before, and the trick would no longer work on him.

He started to turn from the window when his attention was snagged by the soft pink glow emanating from a neon silhouette above the strip club across the street. A female silhouette, nude and featureless, no doubt established to encourage thoughts of sex and fantasy. It was a strange thing, he wondered, how a featureless silhouette could lead human beings to stray. Simple lines, burning with neon light, curved and twisted into the shape of a female. Something so simple. Then again, he mused, the Siren's Song was simple. Simple, but effective.

He stared at that silhouette for a time, his thoughts fighting to chase away the fear that threatened to swallow Detective Hale whole. He had never looked at the city as a safe place to be, but he never imagined it would become as dangerous as it had. An elusive serial killer ran loose within it, the man he called Red Crane.

Some in his department believed these murders were the work of multiple suspects. Few took Hale's blood-soaked paper cranes seriously. Even when he set the blood-stained

4

baubles on Chief William's desk, Hale was blown off with prejudice and told to discard the disgusting artifacts. They were all tested and known to contain the blood of the victims the cranes were left behind with. But the paper creations contained nothing that linked back to the killer.

The latest victim was a woman. Her name eluded Hale. He hadn't paid that much attention to her file, only knew that she had her throat slit and had bled out across the carpet in the center of the living room.

He huffed before finally turning back to the living area. Moonlight flooded the dark stain in the center of the chevron-patterned rug where the victim had breathed her last. Her body had been taken to the morgue, but the apartment still sat, untouched by investigators. Was the Department so busy it couldn't be bothered to investigate a woman's death that was obviously the work of a killer?

Hale shook his head and took a deep breath, his eyes taking in the room around him. The small apartment was a place Detective Hale saw himself occupying in another life, another time. The one-bedroom suite was the perfect size for a single man living in the city, with a small area for one to sleep, and a small area to entertain guests. A quaint little kitchen fought for its own place in the cramped dwelling, giving just enough room for the appliances, a small table, and a couple barstools.

Detective Hale was not a single man living in the city. He was a detective with a wife and teenage daughter. They lived in a small house in the outskirts of the city, away from the crimes of Jameson. Away from the hustle and the bustle.

Away from Red Crane.

The moniker that Detective Hale attached to his latest murder suspect felt more appropriate the more Hale thought about it. Besides the Crane's calling cards—origami cranes soaked in their victims' blood—Crane had become sort of a crane himself. He had managed to soar out of the grasp of the department's force. In fact, he had become a ghost. After a handful of murder cases with Red Crane's calling card at each one, the further into the case Detective Hale dug, the more elusive his prey became and the more determined Hale became in catching Red Crane. It didn't help that each and every piece of the physical evidence couldn't be traced to a specific individual, making Hale's attempts at capturing this killer nearly impossible. It made him look inept, and so he had been pulled off the case officially, but he continued to scour the crime scenes for evidence in a vain attempt at catching the killer. Nothing could stop Hale.

Apparently, not even death.

Hale reached into his coat and felt the scar tissue in the left side of his chest, where he had been stabbed in the heart four months earlier by an unknown figure who jumped him in a dark alley.

"Damn you," he grumbled. He turned toward the kitchen and browsed the random magnets on the refrigerator while he fought to catch his breath. Every now and then his heart would act up, and it only served to remind him that he was neither invincible nor very useful. It didn't help that Hale wasn't exactly in shape. A few pounds overweight, with days of stubble and a mane that needed a cut, he wasn't a poster boy for police fitness.

The magnets were arranged on the fridge in a neat and tidy

order, and each looked shiny and new as if they all had been cleaned with bleach recently. But the magnets - most from local restaurants and a few from tourist locations around the globe - told him nothing about the murder.

The ache in his chest forced him to take a seat in the leather recliner in the living area. He didn't want to rest. He wanted to find the killer. But his body wouldn't let him go too far ahead before reminding him of his mortality.

He took a deep breath and rubbed the scar tissue through his white dress shirt, his mind reeling with the horrible event. Before the incident, Hale had always assumed that a wound to the heart always equaled an instant kill. Not in his case though. It meant a lifetime of medication, pain, and more hospital checkups than one could stomach in a lifetime. It was almost worse than death. Almost.

Detective Hale made it his new mission in this second chance to find Red Crane and put a stop to the insanity plaguing Jameson. The department might shun him for thinking a serial killer was on the loose. His superiors might bring the hammer down on him if he didn't stop undermining them. His wife might even think of divorcing him if he didn't stop obsessing over a twisted serial killer.

He stood to his feet, determined to find and stop Red Crane before he—or she—took more victims.

Hale continued his search around the apartment as he browsed the in-wall bookshelves, scanned the big-screen television, and scoured the small bathroom - which was immaculately clean. Nothing stood out to him, aside from the various toppled items that filled the living space and did nothing but indicate a struggle.

And then his eyes caught sight of the one item he had been searching for, the one item that would connect his assumptions with the truth of the matter. Atop the small end table that stood in the shadows near the overturned couch perched a small origami crane made of paper.

Hale took a pair of tweezers from the inside pocket of his overcoat and used them to lift the crane from its pedestal. He examined the paper bird under the moonlight and noticed that it was nearly identical to the other paper birds. The crane was soaked in blood, no doubt the victim's.

The calling card of Red Crane.

 **ONE**

Thursdays were the worst. So close to Friday, but not quite there. So far from Monday, but with Monday's unfinished projects lingering in the air. Detective Hale hated Thursdays, especially when he hadn't been able to gain any solid sleep the night before.

By the time he arrived home at three in the morning, his wife was already in a deep sleep. Since she usually suffered from acute insomnia, Hale left her alone and climbed into the bed next to her, dozing off almost immediately. But his slumber only lasted two hours before he had to wake and head into the office to continue his pursuit of Red Crane. He had to leave before his wife woke. Most times she didn't even know he had come home and then left again. And as much as he would have liked to have woken her up for an early morning 'rendezvous', he didn't dare rob her of precious sleep, a commodity that she cherished above all else. It was rare for her to sleep a solid four hours during the night, so when she was asleep, he did his best to not bother her.

Sometimes days would go by without them having any kind of mutual interaction. He saw her asleep. She saw him asleep. When they saw each other, they fought. Fought about Red Crane. Fought about the lack of sex and communication in their relationship. Fought about their daughter. Fought about every and anything.

His only sanctuary lately seemed to be the police precinct.

Detective Hale set his cup of coffee down on the only free surface of his desk amid the stacks of paperwork, folders of debriefings, and take-out containers. It was the fourth coffee cup on his desk, and most of the others were at least half full of cold coffee from the same vending machine in the break room.

"Hale?"

He turned to the scratchy female voice to his right. Stephanie was already at her desk, having probably finished five assignments before the sun even rose. Her desk, he noticed, was immaculate. Not a scrap of trash. The smell of furniture polish filled the air. How she was so clean and efficient was beyond him.

"Hale?" she asked again, tilting her head to match his gaze. Her large blue eyes sparkled under the fluorescent lights.

He shook his head and gave her a solemn wave before sitting down at his landfill of a workspace.

Even though five feet existed between their desks, Stephanie managed to lean over the expanse and, in a conspiratorial tone, asked, "What are you doing here?"

The faint scent of vanilla carried off her person and invaded his messy space. "My job," he answered loudly before pushing the power button on his computer. He rubbed his cheek, and the stubble reminded him he hadn't shaved.

"I heard they took you off Red Crane's case."

Hale powered on his computer monitor and began rummaging through the refuse on his desk. He tossed the take-out food containers in the small metal wastebasket he kept underneath his desk. He piled all of the manila debriefing folders in a semi-neat stack to the left of this monitor. Then he piled all of the loose paperwork together and slid it off the surface of his desk into the wastebasket, all but a small yellow note he didn't recognize. It was weighed to the desk with a silver bangle.

Hale picked up the square posty note. In thick black ink, **James 1:15** had been written. "Did you leave this on my desk, Steph?"

She glanced over to the note in his hand and shook her head. "I don't have posty notes that color." She leaned over and took a closer look at the note and then glared at him. "And you know I don't believe in that nonsense."

"Nonsense?"

She nodded as she returned to her upright position. "The Bible. Fairy tale stuff."

"I suppose so," Hale said, lying to himself. "Just the same, who left this here? How did it get on my desk? And what's with this bracelet?" He lifted the heavy silver bangle. Green gemstones were inlaid all around the outside in the shape of little emerald stars. It seemed familiar to him, but he couldn't place it.

She shrugged. "It's not mine."

Hale stuck the note to the side of his monitor and placed the bracelet in the top drawer of his desk. Then he leaned back in his chair and took a good long look at his workspace. A smile crept across his face. It was nice to see something productive come out of his work at the precinct.

"If Chief Williams sees you here…"

Hale sighed and then turned his chair so he was facing her. He was surprised to find her wearing the same black shirt she had worn the day before. She loved wearing black. He always

11

thought of ravens when he saw her in black. Today she also wore makeup—simple eyeshadow, and lipstick that came out in a pinkish hue. Her eyes were a bright cerulean, filled with whirlpools of deep ocean. They were eyes he had to be careful not to get lost in.

"I'm not worried about it," he answered her. "After all the cases I've solved for this precinct, the least Chief Williams can do is leave me alone."

"You think that's the least I can do?"

Hale spun his chair around and came face to stomach with Chief Williams. The man had a gargantuan gut – probably filled with pasta—and he was tall to boot. "Sir."

"Come to my office, Hale," he growled. "Now." He turned and sauntered back to the small glass box in the corner of the room.

Hale grinned at Stephanie, who gritted her teeth nervously, and then he followed the Chief. Once in the office, the man motioned for Hale to close the door behind him. Hale did so and then took a seat in the old green chair that he had sat in one too many times, especially over the course of the last few months.

Williams clasped his meaty hands together on the desk and sighed. "You know what I'm going to say, don't you?"

"You can't, sir," Hale replied as he gripped the back of his neck and attempted to work out a knot in his muscle. "I'm close. I can feel it."

"Damn it, Hale. I can't keep the big guys off your back anymore. My boss is coming down on me like a pile of bricks, and you keep handing him the shovel."

Hale leaned forward in his chair and took a deep breath. The air in Chief Williams' office stunk of cigars and basil. "Do you believe Red Crane is real?"

Williams pointed his finger at Hale. "You're treading dangerous crowd, Detective. You know what I think. You know what I believe. You know that I've been fighting to keep you in this ring for as long as I could. But I have so much hot breath on my neck, I can't pee without sweating. I gave you ample warning to leave the Red Crane cases alone. You refused…and so forced my hand."

Hale leaned back in the chair and let out a deep sigh. He took notice of the family portraits gracing the wall behind Williams. The man's wife looked the polar opposite of him: skinny, blonde, and somewhat calm. Williams always had a red tint to his face.

"Sorry," Williams said as he held his hands out. "Badge and gun. Now."

Hale removed his sidearm and his badge. He took a long look at them before he set them down on the desk and watched Williams slide them away. Then he stood up and went straight to the door.

"Hale?" Williams beckoned.

Hale opened the door and looked out on the floor to where Stephanie was sitting. She was busy at work on her computer terminal, probably typing in reports. Always reports.

He turned to Williams. "What?"

"I have a friend…someone who might be able to help you in your…quest."

"Who?"

"He's known as Germaine. He lives in a concrete building downtown. He sees all. Might know something about your Red

Crane."

"Great. Is it safe to go down there without a gun?"

Williams stroked his cheeks. Hale could see a faint patch of stubble hiding in the folds of fat, but nothing as thick as what was currently growing on Hale's own face. "Take Stephanie. She's caught up with her cases. I told her to take a few days off to rest and recharge and she refuses. I'll send her with you, off the clock."

Hale nodded. Then he turned and went back to his desk to retrieve the Red Crane file he had been working on for the last six months.

Stephanie leaned over and whispered, "What did the Chief want?"

"My badge and gun," Hale said. "But in return, he gave me you. C'mon, we're going downtown."

Stephanie's ocean eyes filled with suspicion. "Me?"

Hale nodded as he finished filling the Crane folder with odd notes and photographs. Then he shut down his computer system. "I need backup. There may be a lead on Red Crane."

"Geez, Hale. How did you manage to get suspended AND get Chief Williams to let me help you?"

Hale shrugged. He truly didn't know. All he did know was that he wanted nothing more than to find Red Crane and to put things back in order.

 **TWO**

The stench of urine and alcohol bit at the air, smells Hale was used to working in the city. Still, he covered his nose with the collar of his trench coat. Stephanie wore a long white overcoat, and a white knit beanie that was big enough to cover her ears. A heavy perfume air surrounded her, one that reminded Hale of what his wife usually spritzed on the nights they engaged in amorous activities. Vanilla.

The alley leading to 'Germaine's Place'—as the destitute homeless woman Hale gave a loaf of bread to for information had called it—was thick with darkness. The brick walls of the two industrial buildings creating the alley were marred with various sprays of graffiti and stains of blood and other foul things. The buildings had been abandoned after having been nearly destroyed by the Riots of New Hamburg years earlier. Hale remembered those riots, as they had been the catalyst to him meeting his wife. She was a reporter, and he a cop. Paths crossed. Planets aligned. History had been written.

He also remembered this alley. It was the same alley he had engaged in a rendezvous with one of his illicit affairs months earlier.

The alley was illuminated by streetlamps that had been placed every couple hundred feet or so. Puddles of rainwater from the previous day's storms filled the numerous potholes

15

in the street, reflecting the ugly orange lamp light. Vehicles rarely traveled through the alleys because of the congestion of garbage bins, old wooden pallets, and haphazardly parked cars.

This late at night, this part of Jameson was mostly abandoned, save for homeless that usually wandered the area. Hale found them to be mostly docile, but he heard rumors of the occasional turf wars between the transients residing underneath the nearby freeway on-ramp and the transients who called these alleys their homes.

Luckily, this particular alley was mostly abandoned for reasons the homeless lady who had given Hale his coordinates said were suspicious. Strange sounds, random vanishings. Eerie things. Particularly in the last few months.

Hale shined his flashlight to the end of the alley where there was supposed to be a brick wall, the other side of which was the freeway. But the light refused to pierce the darkness at the end. Instead, the flashlight beam vanished halfway through the alley, revealing a black fog that seemed to permeate the space between the two buildings.

Despite the darkness, Hale moved forward through the alley, determined to put a stop to Red Crane's killings and to the roller coaster his life had turned into as of late. He wanted his job back, his wife back, his life back. He wanted this murderous psycho off the street, and he wanted the victims avenged.

Stephanie grasped his arm as they moved toward the wall of shadow ahead of them. Her grip was firm, but there was electricity to it, a buzz that made his aching heart jolt. It was this electricity that Hale found intoxicating.

He pulled his arm out of her strong grip and hastened a

few steps ahead of her. The stench of her perfume nearly overrode the dour scent of piss, but not completely. Hale shielded his nose once again with the collar of his jacket. As he moved through the alley, the beam of his flashlight became shorter and shorter, until he couldn't even shine the light far enough to see a few feet in front of him. Even the ugly orange lamps refused to allow their light to venture this far into the corridor.

The air became thicker the further they moved through the alley. Hale's thoughts wandered from the things he would like to do with his wife once Red Crane was caught—hikes, a trip, have another child—to thoughts of how nice it felt to have Stephanie with him in this darkness.

He stopped when he approached an opening in the wall to their right. It looked as if the bricks had been busted out by a sledgehammer to make way for someone three times the size of Hale. Hale noticed streaks of blood outlining the opening.

Stephanie drew her pistol. "That's not a good sign," she whispered. "What do you think caused that?"

Hale shook his head as he drew his gun. He would have thrown a stink about Chief Williams taking his police-issued handgun if he cared about it. In truth, he much preferred his own hand-crafted pistol. He had built it from parts he ordered individually from various manufacturers to specifications he had given the sellers. The gun was made from ultra-light metal alloy and took specialized ammo that was able to spread through a person's body on impact, incapacitating them. Chief Williams hated that Hale used the gun, stating it should be made illegal, but he subjugated himself to Hale's discretion.

As much as Hale conflicted with the man, Hale had a decent

amount of respect for Chief Williams.

Hale stepped through the opening in the wall and shined his flashlight into the old building. From what he understood of this part of Jameson, this building was one of many factories that had at one time been abuzz with manufacturing. Manufacturing that made Jameson more than a dot on a map. Those days were over thanks to the riots and the declining economy.

Darkness filled the space, absorbing the beam from his flashlight.

"Hello?" he called out into the strange void. His voice echoed off the cement walls inside, but no audible response came back to him. The scent of human sewage hit him square in the face and forced him to turn toward the opening in the wall for a breath of fresh air.

"You okay?" Stephanie asked as she stepped through the hole and entered the building. "It's so dark in here."

"We should leave," Hale said. "Something about this place…"

"Yeah," Stephanie replied. "I feel it too. A heaviness."

Hale rubbed his chest. The scar began to ache, so much so that he found himself kneeling in the darkness, his gun slipping from his grip. His chest tightened as an unknown force pressed in on him from all sides.

Stephanie pulled him into the alley and set him on the ground against the opposite wall.

The pain in Hale's chest intensified, making it difficult to catch his breath. "I think I might need—"

A slow hiss seeped out of the hole in the wall.

Stephanie raised her weapon toward the opening. "Jameson

P.D. Come out of there!"

"Hale." The words formed, lending life to the dark cloud botching up the whole alley: "Sin is death."

Hale's stomach threatened to toss out the contents of his latest meal—noodles and fried rice. He glanced up at the dark hole which seemed to be swallowing up everything around it and saw a pair of glowing red eyes. Hale tried to lift his weapon but realized he didn't have it, then he tried to scramble from the wall but couldn't move. The strength had drained from him so quickly. "Who…What…are you?" he whispered.

Stephanie fired a shot into the darkness. The eyes blinked, glowed fire-red, and then grew larger within the darkness, and continued to grow larger until they were taking up the entirety of the dark space. Hale stared into that redness, into those eyes, until the red swallowed him whole.

THREE

W hen his eyes first opened, Detective Hale took the fact that he couldn't hear his clock alarm as confirmation that it wasn't time to wake up yet. He rolled over and sought to return to sleep when he smelled heavy perfume—vanilla—wafting up from the pillow he rested his head on. His mind mistook it for his wife's scent.

The second time his eyes opened, Hale jolted from the bed and scrambled across the room, the pain in his chest pulsing with the unplanned movement. He flipped the switch to the bedroom light and took in the terror he hoped had only been a dream—a red-painted room, a four-post canopy bed, and a tapestry of silk and velvet spread around overtly feminine room decor.

Hale glanced down and found himself still clothed in what he wore before he collapsed in the alleyway in Jameson: slacks and a dress shirt.

"You okay?"

Startled, he looked to the door and gripped his chest. "Why did you bring me back here?"

"You're welcome," Stephanie huffed as she entered the room with a brown tray containing a tall glass of water and a plate of scrambled eggs. She set the tray on the dresser by the door and crossed her arms over her chest. "You blacked out. Back at Germaine's Place."

Hale cautiously took a seat on the edge of the bed and put a hand to his forehead. Slimy perspiration coated his skin. "What happened?"

"You blacked out," she answered again. Hale noticed she had changed into a white night slip which she covered with a long black robe. "I fired some shots into that hole in the wall and those eyes. They disappeared."

Hale huffed. "You didn't take me to a hospital. Or home."

"That's right," she said. Hale recognized a hint of hostility in her voice. "I didn't want to raise suspicion. You're not officially on duty. Neither am I. I can get in a lot of trouble for firing my gun when I'm not on duty, and you can get in trouble because you're supposed to be suspended."

Hale nodded. "Okay. Well," he pulled his sleeve back and checked his watch. Four in the morning. "Dammit. I need to get home."

Stephanie nodded. Then she grabbed the tray of food and left the room. Hale went to the bathroom and checked himself in the mirror. His face was covered in a thin layer of hair. His hair was bedraggled, his locks falling down just above his thick eyebrows. He ran cold water and rinsed his face. Then he used one of her hand towels, a black one with a large 'S' on it, to dry his face. It smelled of her: vanilla. Smelled of his wife.

He glanced around the bathroom. Evidence of Stephanie was everywhere. For some reason, Hale always thought she had a secret boyfriend she never told him about. But it was just *her* toothbrush. *Her* hairbrush. He opened the medicine cabinet and found a slew of various medicine bottles, all with *her* name on them. A box of tampons. A compact. Various bottles of nail polish in a variety of colors. There was a used box of dark brown hair dye in the trash can.

Hale took a deep breath and stared at his reflection in the mirror. "Get out of here," he whispered. "Go home to your wife. Go home to your family. Go home to your future."

Hale left the bathroom and found Stephanie in the bedroom. She stood by the bed, the robe gone, her curves accentuated by the sleeveless night slip. Her legs were ghostly white, and her arms had splotches of freckles up near the biceps. She looked a bit nervous, but stood confident, like a teenage cheerleader trying to seduce the captain of the football team.

He spotted his trench coat on the small, cushioned seat that ran along the wall underneath a multitude of hanging bookshelves. Stephanie stood in front of it, blocking his path. He charged toward the coat, a singular mission in his mind. Before he could reach it, Stephanie stepped in front of him, arms crossed, pushing her breasts up and almost out of the gown. "Are you in a hurry?" she asked in a soft voice.

Hale wanted to move her out of the way, but something deep in his gut told him not to touch her. He had touched enough women, he had wrecked enough of his marriage with infidelity. Stephanie was another girl, a stranger in his long walk of life. He didn't want to get mixed up with her.

She turned and picked up his coat. Then she handed it to him. "Go if you must," she finally said. "But you know you don't have to."

He took his jacket. "I do. I have a wife. A kid."

"But do you have a family?"

Her question startled him. He figured it was obvious that a wife and kid made a family, but the way she was staring at him—her eyes almost pleading for his companionship—told him that she meant something else entirely.

"I have Meranda. I have Brittany." Speaking his wife and daughter's name in this place sent a rock to the bottom of his stomach, as if he had just tainted the holy water in the Sistine Chapel.

She dared to take his hand. He flinched at first. She dared again, and this time he allowed his palm to join with hers. Electricity filled his body. He dropped his jacket on the floor.

She smiled, but her lips were full of bitterness, not warmth. "They do not make a family, Hale. Meranda still doesn't forgive you for what you did. Brittany hates you."

"I slept with another woman. She has a right to not forgive me. And Brittany is just a teenager. She doesn't know what she should feel. But she *should* feel bitter toward me. I screwed everything up. And now I'm trying to fix it all."

Stephanie took hold of his other hand. She pulled him close to her, until her breasts were nearly touching his chest. "It's not a quick fix, Hale." Her warm breath fell on his face, and in it he smelled peppermint. "And do you know if it will even be worth it? What if you deny yourself these simple pleasures only to get to the end and find that Meranda has left you? Or that Brittany has disowned you? Will it be worth it?"

"I don't know," is all he could think of saying.

"I'm your partner, Hale. Your friend. I've been with you in some pretty tight spots. You trust me, don't you? Your friend?

Your partner?"

He felt her heartbeat resonating through her breasts and into his chest, as if they were conduits to her sexual energy.

"You are my friend," he finally said. "My partner." The trust he had placed in her during their career together - however short-lived it had been - was a kind of trust he couldn't even place in Meranda. Fear drove him each morning, out of his bed and back into the job. Fear that Meranda would do the same to him that he had done to her - cheat and back-stab. Would she wait until their relationship was restored to turn the tables on him, cut him when his emotions allowed access to his innermost vulnerabilities?

Stephanie released his hands, but he never felt a break in the electric signal she was sending him with her flesh. She slid the straps of the night slip from her shoulders and allowed the thin fabric to float to the floor.

Much like the red eyes, Hale found himself falling into the darkness of Stephanie's presence.

*****

The third time Hale opened his eyes, it was to his ringing phone. He reached his arm over the side of the bed and fished through his pants pocket to get it.

"Yes," he answered.

"Hale."

"Chief?"

"I need you to get Stephanie and head to Stork Island."

"A murder?"

"Your friend's handiwork."

"Red Crane?"

"This isn't official business for you, Hale. Look for clues, but don't cause a scene. Have Stephanie make any arrests or handle any evidence you find."

"Understood, sir."

The call disconnected. Hale stared at the display on his phone for a few moments before venturing to the bathroom to wash up. His wife had called twice in the two hours he had fallen into Stephanie.

And so, Hale sealed his fate.

FOUR

Detective Hale and Stephanie arrived on Stork Island long after a police and CSI unit had already taped off the scene and began their lengthy investigation. The cold morning air chilled Hale's lungs, filling them with ice and regret. His wound ached, but what ached more was his conscious. After having slept with Stephanie, he felt numb inside, as if he had no feelings toward Stephanie or his wife. Making love to Stephanie had been euphoric. She was a solid ten years younger than his wife and her body showed it. Her breasts, her thighs, her skin—all of it felt new and fresh and gave Hale the same intense feelings he felt when he had relations with the women he slept with months earlier.

But the euphoria wore off quick, and he was always left with pain and guilt. What was warm and embracing quickly turned cold and hollow.

Stephanie was not indifferent towards him after the act like the others he had slept with. She strove to remain in his embrace just a little longer, even pulling him back into the bed next to her when he tried to get up to go to the bathroom. Her actions told him that she truly cared for him. Not love, per se, but at least he wasn't a one-night-stand to her.

Unfortunately, she would have to be a one-night-stand to

him. His wife waited at home for him.

"Hale?"

He snapped out of his reverie and found himself staring across the Bay to the city of Jameson. The lights of the city buildings had begun to fade as the sun started its slow climb through the morning fog.

He turned to Stephanie. "Yeah."

She beckoned him to follow her. She seemed different now in the same black shirt she wore every day on the job. It seemed strange not to see her in the night slip, or in nothing at all. It was as if she had to put up a barrier now in the real world. A wall so others wouldn't see her for who she was. But Hale knew none of that was true. She was always transparent and honest with herself and others. It was a trait he had come to appreciate the most about her.

Hale followed her as they crested a moist grassy knoll and came down to a warehouse that looked to have been abandoned by fishermen long ago. Beat up and dismantled motorboats lay derelict around the wooden building. The smell of dew-covered grass and Bay air filled Hale with a strange dread. Night was over and morning had come, despite him wishfully believing morning would never come.

Stephanie took him inside the warehouse where a cluster of large metal hooks, rusted and creaking, hung from the A-frame. One particular hook, large and bloodied, had a body hanging from it. The hook pierced through the victim's back and came out the front of his collarbone. Blood soaked the man's shirt and had collected in a puddle on the floor near where Hale stood.

"Red Crane," Hale whispered. "Could he get anymore gruesome?"

"Hale? Don't you recognize him?"

Hale glanced up with the help of the police flood lights and tried to put a name to the face, but the body kept spinning as the hooks moved like a school of slow-moving fish. In the right slice of light, he finally caught a glimpse of the victim's face – Detective Auburn.

"Why?" Hale asked aloud.

Stephanie shrugged. "He just barely joined the force a few weeks ago."

Hale nodded. "Good kid."

"Yeah," Stephanie agreed. "I know he looked up to you."

Hale was surprised to learn of the man's admiration. Williams had put Hale in charge of taking Auburn around Jameson on his first few days to show him around and give him a run-down of how the different districts of Jameson operated. They had lunch in Jameson. They met some…side entertainment in the Strikt District. They even crossed Lark Bridge and spent some time goofing around in Foster City. Hale didn't usually like playing tour guide, but Auburn had a pleasant personality and a kind disposition, something Hale didn't see too often in this city.

"Well…let's get him down." Hale glanced around the warehouse and found the Red Crane's calling card sitting on a wooden table with a yellow evidence number next to it. A blood trail went from the puddle underneath Auburn to the blood-soaked origami crane on the table. This was the first time that Hale had seen the Red Crane become sloppy with his work. He knew the cranes were always soaked in the blood of the victims, but he had never seen a physical indicator of it like the blood trail.

Henry, one of the crime scene investigators, pointed to the crane. "Same calling card, isn't it?"

Hale looked at the bespectacled man and nodded. Henry was someone Hale had grown fond of throughout the Red Crane's crime spree because he was a man of detail and a man who loved his job.

"That's a shame," Henry said. "Auburn was a good kid. A bit misled...but a good kid."

"Misled?" Stephanie asked.

"Oh yeah. I caught the kid cheating on his wife last week. We were called to an unrelated murder in the Strikt District. Kid was screwing around with one of the corner dames. I told him to knock that shit off, but I caught him again a few days ago when I was called to a domestic issue over in the same district." Henry shook his head. "Damn shame. If I had his wife—fine looking doll—I wouldn't be cheating with anyone."

Hale gazed up at the turning body and wondered for a brief moment if it was his own 'tour' of the Strikt District that had prompted Auburn to return there. It seemed too perfect to be a coincidence.

Stephanie drew beside him and gingerly put her hand on his back. He did nothing to remove it. "You okay?" she asked.

He squared his jaw. "I want to find this sonuvabitch and put an end to this."

 **FIVE**

Morning bled across the sky much like Red Crane's victims bled – quickly. Too quickly. Hale felt his insides fill with coal as he made his way into Oaks City. When he arrived at his quaint little house in the outskirts of the flashier Jameson, Hale killed the engine but sat in the car, his mind berating him for sleeping with Stephanie. He had slept with other women before, but something about this particular instance felt different. Felt wrong. Well, wronger than wrong.

He stepped out of the car, regret making the driveway pavement under his feet slippery and hazardous. As he trudged toward the one-story ramshackle of a house, he realized the air suddenly smelled good. Fresh-cut lawn. A fireplace burning somewhere in the neighborhood. Exhaust. So much exhaust. The smells of morning. The smells of life. The smells reminded him he was alive, but they in turn reminded him that he was dead. Dead in his relationship with his wife. Dead in spirit.

Hale used his key to enter the house.

Seconds after he stepped foot across the threshold and entered the foyer, Meranda came around the corner from the family room and set an overflowing cardboard box down on the tile floor near his feet. "Take it," she said, "and get the hell out of my house."

Hale was in the middle of taking off his trench coat when the words stabbed him in the chest. He jolted his arms up to get his coat back to his shoulders, and then he stood there, staring into her bloodshot eyes. "Have you been crying?" was all he could say.

She wiped her nose on the sleeve of her flower-print nightgown, sniffled, and then pointed to the box. "This is all I'm giving you right now. Come back later for the rest when Brittany and I aren't here."

He reached out toward her, but she took two steps back, shaking her head. "What did I do?" he asked. As soon as the words left his mouth, he realized the answer. Meranda was holding up a pair of lady's panties. Red. Lace. He couldn't remember whose they were.

She dropped the underwear in the box and grimaced. "I don't want to know her name. I don't want to know who she is or where she came from or anything else. Nothing else. I just...I just want you out. You messed up, Hale. You messed up, and I gave you another chance. And now this? I find these in our home, in MY bed?!"

Hale took a step back and bumped up against the front door which he had mistakenly closed after entering the house. He briefly wondered if she knew about Stephanie. About where he had been all night.

Brittany peered around the corner from the living area, her wide blue eyes pleading with her father.

Meranda caught Hale staring behind her and turned to address their teenage daughter. "Your father's not here to stay."

Brittany crept out of the living area and rushed to Hale,

wrapping him in a tight hug. "I miss you."

Hale's heart nearly broke. He hugged his girl, unsure of what was really happening. He kissed her forehead and watched tears stream down her cheeks.

"Go back into the living room, Brittany. Your father has to go."

Hale wondered if his daughter understood Meranda's implications. He was pretty sure she had never found out about his previous misgivings, but he wasn't all that certain Meranda hadn't filled their daughter in to paint him as the villain.

Brittany wiped the tears from her cheeks and retreated to the living area.

Meranda crossed her arms over her chest. "Go. Don't come back unless we're gone. You know our schedule. God knows you know our schedule. You probably tattooed it on your ass so you'd know when you could bring your bitches over. Everyone, Hale. Everyone is connected, aren't they? Your job, the city, these women…these women you bring to OUR house. You tie all of this-this chaos together. You tie it all together and you want me and Brittany to go along with it all. Just become oblivious to your uncontrollable desires. No. I tried to keep my faith in this…faith that you would change. That you would do the right thing. No. I won't be that woman who stands by while her unfaithful husband corrupts their family, their household, their lives. Your job was enough to deal with. Your first cheating streak was even worse—but my mercy was enough to give you another chance. But now this? Absolutely not."

Hale opened his mouth, but before a breath could leave his lungs, Meranda was on him. She slammed her palm into his chest, pain echoing throughout his entire body, and he hit the door with a thud. She growled into his face as she brought her lips close to his left ear. "How dare you defile our home like this. I gave you a second chance. More than most men get. Go be with your job or with your partners or with the whole damn city for all I care. Don't say sorry. Don't justify it. Just go."

Once she stepped back and gave him enough room, he took a deep breath to steady the pain in his chest. Then he knelt and picked up his box of prepackaged stuff. His back and knees ached when he rose with the heavy box. He turned, tears running down his face, and walked out of what used to be his sanctuary.

 **SIX**

The cup of coffee on Hale's desk had been there since twelve noon the day before. After Meranda kicked him out, he wandered the city of Jameson most of the day, mostly in a daze. He now figured that he was the link between these murders, but he wasn't certain how.

The maid murdered in her apartment. She was a woman Hale had slept with during a drunken stupor months ago. Harvey, a young man who witnessed Hale holding hands with another woman when he knew that Hale was married to Meranda, Harvey's teacher. The young and impressionable Detective Auburn who had taken a page directly out of Hale's twisted theology and slept around the city of Jameson.

Each of them had a connection, however weak it seemed, to Hale. A connection to his amorous affairs.

Hale stared at the photos before him. He had all eight of them out on the desk before him. Each a headshot of a woman he had slept with in the last six months. If the connection between the murder victims was his amorous lifestyle, it seemed logical to tag Red Crane's mystery identity on one of his past lovers. Most of them had alibis for most of the murders. The maid, the brunette in the photograph to his right, was one of the victims. The blonde directly in front of him, her blue eyes staring out at him with lurid appeal, had left town to spend time with an aunt in the central valley during two of the murders. The woman with the burn wounds on her face had hospital appointments. The woman with the short hair and the nose ring had been working in the Strikt District. Most of the women had alibis. In fact, all of them had places they were at, and proof of such, except for two.

One of those two stared back at him from her desk. Stephanie. She had been staring at him most of the morning after Hale told her to leave him alone. She had no alibis for the murders. All she told him was that she was here at the precinct or at home, alone, watching movies. Her time here at the precinct was usually during hours nobody else was here to confirm her presence, aside from the security check-in, which had unreliable records because of the idiot who worked the desk.

Hale dug his wallet out of his back pocket and slid out a well-worn photo of his wife. Her black hair framing her beautiful face, he set the photo down in the middle of the rest of the women. There was something poetic, something agonizing about putting her photo atop the rest. Something ironic.

Meranda had no alibi for the majority of the murders either. The ones she did have were weak, such as her presence at a laundromat or visiting her mother in Ceradale across Lark Bridge.

Hale ran his hands over his face. He felt the wrinkles there, the age and the wear. He felt sleep pulling at his mind. A hand rested upon his shoulder, and he nearly jumped. He turned to tell Stephanie to leave him alone again, but stopped with mouth agape when he realized it was Chief Williams, with his giant potbelly nearly pressing close to his face.

"How you holding up, Hale?" he asked.

Hale turned away from the man and took another good look at the photographs. "Nothing to be proud of, sir," he said with a level of shame in his voice.

Williams grunted. "We're not in the business of ethics or morals, Hale. Just justice."

"They go hand in hand," Hale mumbled.

"If you're dealing in absolutes, yes. But I don't deal in absolutes, Hale. I deal in the facts. That's all you're called to as a detective. Look at the facts. One of these women has to be your killer if the murders are all linked to your side rendezvous. Forget about why you slept with them or what your wife thinks of it. You have to focus on who would want you dead and how we can prove it."

The phone rang. Hale ignored it as he had been for the last few hours. Williams gave Stephanie a sidelong glance. She huffed and picked up her phone. Hale paid no attention to what was said. He was drowning in the gazes of the women before him. Each photograph gave him a glimpse into their eyes, into their faces. And it was then that he realized that aside from his wife and Stephanie, he knew none of them. He could describe their bodies, the types of undergarments each wore, what perfume each one wore, or the strange scars or moles he had stumbled upon while exploring their flesh. But he couldn't tell anything else about them. What were their hobbies? What were their lifelong dreams? Had any of them ever stared death in the face? Had any of them ever had to make a decision that altered the course of their lives?

Stephanie set the phone down and stood up from her desk.

Hale turned to her and noticed that her face had transformed to a shade of pale under the dim lighting of the precinct.

Chief Williams crossed his arms and sighed. "Let me guess? Another murder. Red Crane?"

Stephanie nodded, her frown trembling as she made her way to Hale's desk. Hale scooped the photographs into a pile and then shoveled them into the top drawer of his desk. "Let's go," he said.

Stephanie put her hand on his shoulder and pressed him down into his chair. Her strength was surprising. "You better let me and Williams handle this one," she whispered.

"I don't work the field very often," Williams said. "It's okay if you want to take Hale."

Stephanie shook her head. "It's Meranda. She's dead."

SEVEN

When they pulled up to the one-story house, Hale didn't wait for the car to stop before he bolted out of the passenger side of the police cruiser and jaunted across the front lawn toward the doorway he had been cast through the day before.

The air didn't smell as good as it had the day before. The lawn carried the stench of dog feces. Instead of fireplace smoke, he smelled rot. And the exhaust that usually carried through the city of Jameson felt heavy in his lungs. Nothing made him feel alive. He only felt death's clutches wrapping around him, its icy touch reminding him of his mortality.

The cloudy sky above their home threatened rain, but that would have been too merciful. Hale loved the rain, and he knew he was never going to get back any of the things he loved.

He found the front door open. Detectives were already scouring the house for clues. There in the foyer, his wife lay on the floor, her throat slit, a blood-soaked paper crane sitting atop her unmoving chest like a hood ornament. Her arms were straight along her sides, and her legs were positioned straight as well.

"Someone posed her that way," the CSI photographer said as a bright flash went off in Hale's face.

Hale grabbed the front of the camera and pushed the man

back a few steps. "No shit, Fernandez." Hale bent down and studied his wife's corpse. Her eyes were closed. Peaceful. The site of her form under such grisly circumstances made him ill, but he pressed on knowing he had to catch this killer. He felt consumed with the thought of Red Crane still being on the loose.

Aside from the long slit in her throat, there were no other indications Red Crane cut her elsewhere. Hale gently lifted her wrists to find no indication of bruising or bleeding. The coppery stench of blood filled the air. Splayed blood had scattered the front of her white sweater. A trail of blood went from her neck to the place where the origami crane sat upon her chest.

He glanced around the foyer and saw nothing out of place. Everything was exactly as he remembered seeing it the day before.

He smelled Stephanie before she knelt before him, investigating the body. Her vanilla scent lent a sour stench to the site of death and decay. It didn't smell as lovely as it usually did, and the foul odor did a number on making his stomach queasier. He turned and upchucked across the tile floor. Stephanie instinctively covered her nose and mouth.

Chief Williams stepped through the doorway, his stone expression revealing that he was unphased by the sights and smells. He knelt on the other side of Meranda to investigate the scene for himself. "I'm sorry, Hale."

Hale said nothing, only stared at the corpse of his wife for a very long minute until Chief Williams and Stephanie vanished elsewhere into the house. This woman on the floor before him had been the mother of his child, his lover, his friend. He examined her face, the angelic curves of her cheeks, the pronounced chisel of her nose. It all seemed so alien to him, and yet, in the back of his spirit, it all felt familiar. This was a woman he been married to, and yet it was a woman he didn't know, hadn't known for months. Years, maybe.

It had been a long, drawn-out decline into unfaithfulness, but he only just now saw it that way. He had been led down a dark road of temptation and had willingly followed. And this is where it had brought him—the death, the murder, of his wife.

Hale pulled a pair of tweezers from the inside pocket of his trench coat and used them to gently grip one of the wings of the blood-drenched paper crane. He lifted it off his wife's chest and pulled it close to his face to inspect it. Knowing that the paper had absorbed a good amount of his wife's blood made him ill, but this time he fought back the urge to retch.

Nothing about the crane stood out to him—not the folds of the paper, not the immaculate way a crane had been formed from such a simple device as a sheet of printer paper. As with the other paper cranes, there were no clues besides the victim's blood. No hair. No skin. Nothing.

He set the crane in an evidence baggie he found on the floor, zipped up the baggie, and then handed the baggie to one of the CSI agents.

Hale moved further into the house and found Stephanie and Chief Williams in the kitchen, speaking to one another in hushed tones.

"Where's Brittany?" Hale asked.

They both shrugged. Hale turned to one of the officers who had been in the house before they arrived. "Where's my daughter?"

The officer glanced around the living area as if he were

searching for her, but then shrugged. "I haven't seen her, boss. When we got here, it was just the body in the foyer."

Hale caught hold of the panic that gripped his chest, flooding his old wounds with incredible pain, and shoved it to the side as he rushed through the house, questioning each and every member of the unit that had arrived there to investigate the case. He searched every room, every closet, every hiding spot he knew his daughter would retreat to if she knew an attacker, an enemy, was in the house with them.

He returned to Chief Williams and Stephanie, huffing. "My daughter…My daughter is gone."

Chief Williams whipped around the corner of the island counter and grabbed Hale by the shoulder. "Calm down. We'll find her, Hale. I promise you that."

"But what condition will she be in when we do?" Hale asked grimly.

"Calm down," Chief Williams reiterated.

An officer entered the kitchen with a small laptop open in his arms. "Guys, I found this in the upstairs bedroom." He set it down on the island counter. Hale recognized it as his daughter's. He glanced at the screen. An email was open, from an unknown sender.

I can't wait to finally meet you in person. Crier Park is beautiful this time of night. Meet you by the oak tree.

Hale took a deep breath and steadied himself. The pain spilled from his chest across the rest of his body. His vision blurred, and he felt sharp pains shooting through his left arm.

Williams reached out to steady him, but Hale waved him away. "I'm fine."

"The oak tree?" Stephanie asked. "There's dozens of oak trees in Crier Park."

Hale turned to leave when Stephanie grabbed her coat off the back of the kitchen chair. "I'll go with you," she said.

He stopped and turned toward her, speaking to her but eying Chief Williams. "I do this on my own."

Williams nodded.

Stephanie threw her hands up in frustration. "You're going to go after a serial killer by yourself?"

Hale left the house.

It would be the last time he ever stepped foot in that house.

 **EIGHT**

Detective Hale refused to allow his foot to let up on the gas as he sped through downtown. He barely missed a semi-truck doing its nightly deliveries and morbidly wondered how ironic it would be if he killed himself trying to save his daughter from a serial killer.

The city skyline was quiet at this late hour, but it didn't mean it was deserted. Various patches of homeless peered out of alleyways and abandoned parking lots. Hale had visited many of these groups in the past to question the homeless on various murder and kidnapping cases. They were the eyes and ears of the city and were often overlooked by most detectives and law enforcement.

Hale usually had the radio blaring when he was in pursuit. It always relaxed his mind. But not tonight. Tonight, he realized he wanted nothing more than to get his daughter back. She was all he had left.

You have Stephanie.

No, he reminded himself. *No, not Stephanie. Nobody.*

He arrived at Crier Park within a half hour of leaving his house. After pulling his vehicle into one of the many empty spots in the parking lot, he double checked his pistol to make sure it was loaded, determined to finally put Red Crane down once and for all. The cold night air seeped quickly into the car, chilling him. He let out a breath and it came out as fog.

"Hale, this is Stephanie. Do you read? Hale, please pick up."

Hale took hold of his CB radio and flipped the power switch to the OFF position. It was the third time Stephanie had tried to hail him on the radio.

He left the car and entered the park underneath the curved archway that had 'Crier Park' twisted in black iron. The park had been a part of the city since before Hale was born, and it was a place that had a twisted sort of meaning and significance to him. He shared his first kiss here when he was sixteen to Meranda…and subsequent kisses after, some of which were with women he barely knew while he was married to Meranda.

That fact was tainted though in light of the truth that this was where he had his very first amorous rendezvous. By the oak tree.

Hale walked a few feet through the entrance of the park and stopped. Fog and cold filled the park. The cement path before him was set out in a straight line that cut directly through the park and stopped at the small man-made lake that resided at the other end of the property. He couldn't see the lake. He had been to the park enough times to know it was there. He wouldn't need to go that far, anyway. The oak tree was to the east from where he stood, a few yards away.

The park was shrouded in darkness, save for a few lamps that, surrounded by fog, lit the path before him in a soft glow. He remembered there being more lighting, but he couldn't be sure.

He turned to the right, in the direction of the oak tree. The darkness was thick, and the dense fog was moving through the park like a live entity, sweeping across the lamps like wraiths. He could feel the moisture in the air settling on his face, in his lungs. He breathed the chill in and felt his lungs thank him for the clean, early morning air.

Hale started off the path across the grass field toward the direction of the tree. He scanned the park as he went, unable to spot much of anything through the darkness and the fog. If the Red Crane was here, he was surely lying in wait.

If his daughter was here, he hoped she was alive.

He jogged, his chest wound squirming in the discomfort of such an action, until he was close enough to see the silhouette of the massive oak just yards in front of him. The fog broke before him, allowing him a straight passageway to the tree. The darkness crept up on both sides of him, creating walls of despair, blocking out all light in the park and beyond. Ahead of him, the tree glowed a strange vanilla color, as if was illuminated by a supernatural ambient light.

As Hale drew closer to the tree, his heart sank. There on the ground, illuminated by the tree's uncanny glow, her body broken and bent across the mighty oak's roots, Hale's daughter bled out from multiple wounds that soaked her violet-colored sweatshirt and blue jeans in dark stains.

A blood-soaked paper crane rested on her chest.

He cradled her head in his arms. Blood leaked out of her mouth and the deep gashes in her face, coating his hands in the sticky substance. She had no breath, no pulse. Her body wouldn't stop leaking blood.

Hale cried as he cradled her pierced form. His vision clouded with tears. So many tears.

He didn't realize until many minutes later that he was sobbing loudly. His crackling voice would have echoed throughout the park were it not for the oppressive fog that had moved in behind him, boxing him in there at the base of the tree.

He gently placed his daughter's head on a particularly massive root that bulged from the ground, and then he stood to his feet. His legs wobbled, and his head swam. He drew his weapon and addressed the fog. "Face me, Crane."

The fog shifted, smoky tendrils drifting in various directions as if someone was moving through it.

"Face me, monster!"

The fog stilled. A low wheeze escaped the darkness. "Who is the real monster here, Hale? Who is the proprietor of these deaths? Of this darkness?"

"You. You are the reason my wife died. You are the reason my daughter lies here dead. You!"

Hale raised his gun and realized his hands were trembling. He steadied himself. Took a deep breath. He tried to steady his footing around the roots of the massive tree, worrisome of the way it glowed. The pain in his chest again reminded him he was not invincible. This could very well be where he himself left this world and faced his judgement.

"Do you think I did this?" the voice asked.

Hale fired off a round. The bullet vanished into the dark fog, as did the sound of the gunshot.

"You would kill me? But can you?"

Hale fired off three more rounds. They each vanished into the fog.

"I cannot be bested. Not here."

"Why? Why did you do it? Why did you kill them? All of them? The maid. The agent. My wife. My daughter?"

"Because you allowed me to."

Hale fired two more rounds into the darkness, but they ended with the same fate as the ones before them.

"There is no way to destroy me…creator."

"I didn't create you. You murdered those people on your own."

"Yes, I guess I did. I guess I was out of control, so to say. But you were the one who created me. Created this chain of events. How is your heart, Detective Hale? Beyond belief, you survived my attempt on your life."

"Stop talking. Come here into the light so I can see you. Come into the light so I can finish this once and for all."

"No. Light cannot exist with me. You still don't get it, do you? You still don't understand any of this."

Hale sensed the fog moving in closer, but at a very slow pace. As it inched closer, as the darkness closed him in more and more, the pressure on his chest increased, making it difficult to breathe.

"I will help you to understand, Hale. Because you and I are going to be together for quite a while. You created me, but you cannot destroy me."

He lowered the gun and knelt near the tree, near his daughter. He glanced at her bloody form and at the blood-soaked crane once more before the lamp post flickered out and the fog consumed him.

NINE

W hen Hale awoke, it wasn't in the park at the oak tree. It wasn't near his daughter's corpse. It was in the past, at the event that changed everything…

Rain fell. The sound of liquid drops splattering against the tin roof woke him from slumber. The sun had just risen, and a cold chill moved through the small house. Hale turned on his side to seek warmth under the bed sheets and found her naked body lying next to his. Her eyes were closed, and he could hear a soft mewling from her throat as she slept. The sheets had fallen off of her chest and revealed a supple pair of breasts. The same breasts he spent the night caressing.

Hale rubbed the sleep from his eyes and fought to remember everything. The bar. The bar was where he went after he and Meranda had their argument. Another argument. It was all they ever did anymore. Argue. Argue because Hale's job took up most of his time. Argue because Hale ignored her sexually and emotionally when he was home. Argue because it was all they knew how to do nowadays.

The woman next to him…he met her at the bar. She wore a tight gray skirt and a loose—very loose—black blouse. A silver bangle with encrusted emeralds slid around on her thin wrist. There was something in her eyes, some kind of wild instinct or energy that he hadn't seen in a lot of people. It was what drew him to her. He knew he shouldn't, knew he shouldn't look at her, talk to her, or even entertain the lurid thoughts that entered his mind of the things he'd like to do with that skirt and that blouse.

But he did. He did do those things after he looked at her—rather stared, and he talked to her, and then he followed her down the street to the park, to the oak tree, where they made out for an hour before a security guard kicked them out. They returned here to her home in the east side of the Bay where most of the trailer trash resided, and they indulged in each other the rest of the night.

After sex, after she fell asleep, Hale watched her stir. She pulled the blankets over her naked form and turned her back to him before she went back to snoring. Her tattoo was clearly visible in the morning light: a paper crane.

Hale left feeling queasy.

When he returned home later that night after a long day of work, he made sure to ignore Meranda. He couldn't let her find out about his affair. So he ignored her. Until she apologized to him for arguing. Then he nodded, hugged her, and spilled out his heart which had filled with the poison of guilt, admitting his grave mistake.

Meranda forgave him, somewhat reluctantly and through a lot of heartache. They went to counseling. They agreed to work on things.

Months later, the arguments started again. Hale ignored her. Life went on.

Hale's memory shifted to the maid at the five-star hotel. The one who had interacted with Hale and his second affair.

Hale's memory pushed and stretched and did what it could to call forth the events surrounding the maid. She had walked in on Hale and the unnamed girl tussling around in the hotel bed.

But the maid knew Hale. Knew him because she had worked with his wife months before.

And the others. The other victims. They all knew Hale or Hale's wife. They all knew of Hale's amorous activities.

They were all connected by his sins.

TEN

Hale opened his eyes to sunlight. He found himself outside, the smell of death filling his nostrils. He tried to sit up and received help in the form of a gentle grip under his arm that pulled him to a sitting position. Stephanie knelt in front of him, her ocean eyes full of somber apologies.

Hale leaned his back against the giant oak tree and blinked a few times to allow the morning light to enter his vision. A light fog lingered throughout the park, but there was no sign of the sinister force he had encountered the night before. Through his peripheral vision, he knew his daughter still lay to the left of him, her body still bent over the oak's giant roots, as if she were a sacrifice to the park's patriarch.

Stephanie's gaze moved from Hale to his daughter. A tear streamed down her cheek. "I'm sorry," Stephanie whispered. "I know how much she meant to you." She turned to look at him, her jaw locked. "Did you catch the bastard?"

Hale took a deep breath, his chest no longer hurting. He said nothing.

Stephanie took a seat on the grass opposite him. She wore a short black skirt the color of ravens, and a matching blouse. Her clothes vaguely reminded him of the unnamed girl in the house with the tin roof. The woman—the night—that had started everything.

Stephanie crossed her legs and pulled the front of her skirt down over the space between them. She blushed a bit as she did it, but she didn't embellish the moment. Instead, she looked Hale in the eyes and frowned. "I'm really sorry, Hale." She motioned to his daughter, to the tree. "What happened here?"

Hale pulled up the collars of his overcoat to shield his neck from the chilly breeze that had suddenly moved into the park, pushing the light fog out and the cold in. "It was all me, Stephanie. It was all me."

"What?" A disgusted look bled across her facial features. Her grimace reminded him of the time he told Meranda about his very first affair. "You?" She swallowed a lump in her throat and pointed to his daughter's corpse. "You did this?"

He shook his head. "Not directly, no. But it was my fault."

She shook her head. Her hair was tied in a ponytail, and the back portion of her hair bounced around like party streamers. "I don't understand."

"It was my affair. Well, my affairs."

Stephanie's face flooded with a look of realization. "Oh, an ex-lover? That's what this was all about? He came after you and your family for revenge?"

Hale slowly stood to his feet. His knees hurt from the cold, and his chest began to ache again. "No. Red Crane." he looked down at the blood-soaked crane resting atop his daughter's chest. Tears welled up in his eyes. "My sins."

Stephanie stood, straightening her skirt on her way up. "Your sins?"

He nodded, refusing to break eye contact with the paper

crane. The fact that his own daughter's life blood had now been permanently soaked into the very fabric of the throwaway trinket struck deep into his core. He wiped his running nose on the sleeve of his overcoat before reaching down to retrieve the crane. He gently pushed the paper craft into the pocket of his overcoat and then started past Stephanie.

She grabbed his arm and pulled him toward her. He stared into her eyes, those eyes that he had gotten lost in when he should have been getting lost in his own wife's eyes.

"Don't go," she whispered. "We can get through this together. You and me."

He shook his head and pulled his arm from her grasp. "No."

Hale left the park. He wasn't sure what to do with himself, so he went back to the station and plopped himself at his desk. Most of the officers and detectives were out on calls. Chief Williams was in his office, but aside from a few glances at Hale from within his glass-walled office, he did nothing to disturb Hale.

Hale stared at his dark computer screen, his mind reeling with all of the connections. The maid. The detective. His own wife and kid. All of them connected by his sin, by his lust. By his unfaithfulness to his wife.

His gaze fell on the small scrap of paper he had found on his desk days earlier. He picked it up and uncrumpled it.

James 1:15

Hale opened the bottom drawer of his desk and pulled out a number of binders and training manuals, stacking them on the surface of the desk as he scavenged for the item of interest: his Bible. Hale pulled out the small leatherback tome and set it on his desk before putting the binders and training manuals back into the drawer and shutting it.

The Bible had been a gift to him from his (now late) uncle many years earlier. The cover was caked in dust and a coffee stain Hale was never able to pinpoint the origin of. He opened the book and took a few moments to find the book of James. Then he found the verse:

Then when lust has conceived, it gives birth to sin; and when sin is accomplished, it brings forth death.

EPILOGUE

The crowd gathered in Wilkes Cemetery was small, nearly insignificant, merely a small group of black umbrellas holding back the heavy raindrops falling from a slate-gray sky. Hale noticed he was the only family member connected to Meranda and his daughter, as Meranda's parents had disowned her when she was younger, and Hale had wanted nothing to do with his own dysfunctional family for the last ten years.

A few associates of Meranda's stood in black garb. The minister was from Meranda's church. Stephanie and Chief Williams came, but they kept to themselves in the back of the small gathering. Hale liked it that way. He couldn't bear to be near Stephanie at his own wife's funeral. Who knew if he would ever want to be near Stephanie ever again.

The rain came down in waves as Detective Hale listened to the minister give the eulogy for his wife and daughter. The coffins in front of him seemed unreal to him, and Hale had to keep from wanting to open them again to make sure it was really his wife and daughter who had vanished from this plane of existence.

"They are buried in this ground but lifted to Heaven. They reside with the Lord now, and peace is theirs. Greater peace than we have. Greater peace than we deserve."

Peace. Hale didn't know what that was anymore. Ever since

he had betrayed his wife, guilt had come to live with him each and every minute of each and every day. And the more guilt that piled on him, the more he wanted to be more unfaithful to avoid it. An endless cycle of guilt and sin.

And destruction.

I'm sorry, he thought. *I'm sorry, Lord, for everything. You gave me a beautiful wife. You gave me a beautiful daughter. I threw them in the trash because I was…I was a fool.*

"Though we mourn their deaths," the minister continued, "we will never forget the joy they brought to our lives. The warmth they brought to our spirits. The impact they made on this world."

Forgive me, Hale pleaded. *Forgive me for chasing them. For sleeping with them. For walking through those doors.*

"Honor their memory by living your lives the way the Lord would want you to. These two children of God were saved by grace and walked out their salvation to the very end."

Hale took a deep breath. His chest ached, but no more than usual. He slid his hand into the pocket of his overcoat and retrieved his daughter's blood-soaked paper crane. His intention was to place it on his daughter's coffin before it could be lowered into the ground.

But when he held it in front of him, he saw that the crane was crisp, clean, and void of his daughter's blood. The paper was stunning white—almost blinding—and he had to lower it in his hands to stop from drawing attention from the funeral crowd.

Hale looked down at the paper crane in his hands and saw a small bit of text written in black marker across one of the wings:

Isaiah 1:18

He slid the crane into his pocket and stood, watching as the coffins were lowered into the ground. He hoped within his aching chest that Red Crane was gone, that the murders this being had inflicted on those around Hale were at an end.

Who was Red Crane? The only answer Detective Hale could come up with was that Red Crane was a manifestation of his sins, the destruction affecting everyone even remotely tied collaterally to him and his affairs.

He hoped with every fiber of his being this was over now. With his wife and daughter dead, Hale would need to rebuild his life. And rebuilding it would take strength he knew he didn't have.

He eyed Stephanie across the way, her black dress and veil giving her the form of a dark raven. He would need to watch out for her. Would she die like the others? Would she try to strike a relationship with him now that his wife and child were dead?

Hale blew out a long breath and shoved his hands into the pockets of his overcoat, knowing he couldn't put his energy into her. He had to focus on his own healing if he wanted to continue to be a detective, to help others. There would be no more infidelity. No more carousing.

There would only be his work at helping to uncover truth. It was the only thing he could give anyone now.

Look for more of Detective Hale
in *Black Raven* coming soon!